This storybook belongs to:

....

Retold by Mandy Archer

A catalogue record for this book is available from the British Library

Published by Ladybird Books Ltd
80 Strand, London, WC2R 0RL
A Penguin Company

002
© LADYBIRD BOOKS LTD MMXII
Stories originally published in Ladybird Favourite Stories For Boys © MMXI

ISBN: 978-0-71819-912-8

Printed in China

Ladybird

Traditional Tales for Boys

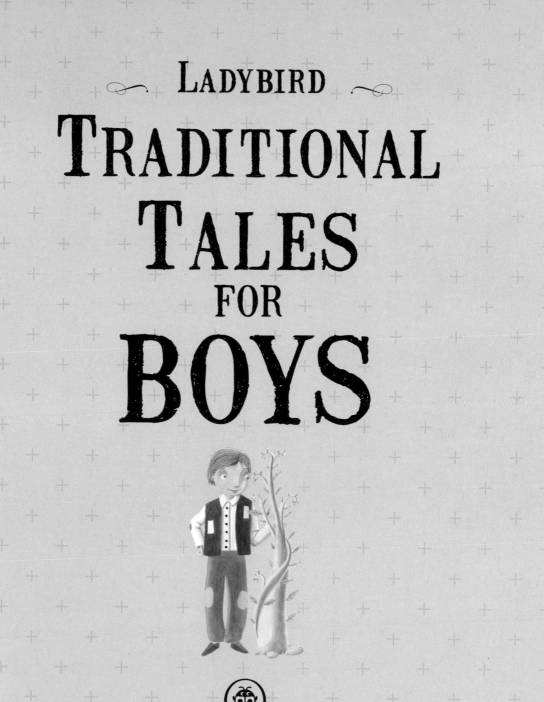

Contents

THE THREE LITTLE PIGS

THE ELVES AND THE SHOEMAKER

THE THREE BILLY GOATS GRUFF

JACK AND THE BEANSTALK

ONCE UPON A TIME there was a widow who lived with her only son, Jack. The pair worked on the land together, but they struggled to make ends meet.

One day, Jack's mother couldn't even afford to buy food for their supper.

"Go to the market and sell our cow," she told her son. "She's the only valuable thing that we have left."

As Jack was walking down the lane, an old man beckoned him over.

"I don't have any money," said the stranger. "But I will give you five magic beans for your cow."

Jack was an honest lad, but he was also lazy. Even though he knew his mother would be cross, the old man's offer was too tempting to resist.

"I can't be bothered to go to the market anyway," he yawned.

Jack took the beans. They seemed ordinary, but what might they grow into?

Jack gave the old man the cow, then walked back to
the cottage.

"Mother!" he cried. "Look what I've brought home."

When his mother saw that Jack didn't have any money,
she was furious.

"Those beans won't feed us, you silly boy!" she scolded.

Jack gasped as she snatched the beans and hurled them out
of the window.

"Now we're sure to starve!" snapped his mother.

Poor Jack went to bed without any supper. But when he woke up the next morning, there was a surprise waiting outside his bedroom window. In the garden, a towering vine was curling up towards the sky.

"It's a beanstalk!" cried the boy, leaping out of bed.

Jack's magic beans had grown into the tallest beanstalk he had ever seen. Jack decided that he had to climb to the very top.

Jack pulled on his clothes, then scrambled
out of the window. He grasped the giant
beanstalk and began to heave himself up.
He kept on climbing until the cottage and
fields below looked very small indeed.
"Come back!" cried Jack's mother, but he
didn't hear her.

When Jack finally reached the top of the beanstalk, he discovered an enormous castle. A giant woman opened the front door.

"Watch out!" she hissed. "My husband will eat you up if he sees you!"

Suddenly there was a thunder of giant footsteps.

Fee-fi-fo-fum,
I smell the blood of an Englishman.
Be he alive or be he dead,
I'll grind his bones to make my bread!"

The woman scooped Jack up and took him inside.

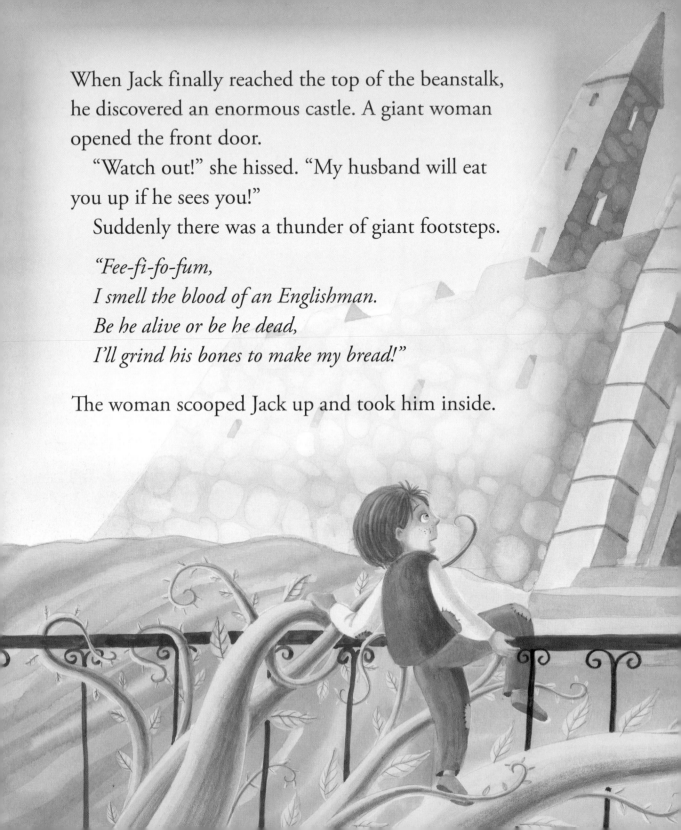

Jack watched from a cupboard as the big, ugly giant slammed fistfuls of money bags on to the kitchen table.

"So many gold coins," he chuckled greedily. "And they're all mine!"

When the giant had finished counting his money, he bellowed for some supper. His wife scuttled in with a pot of broth that was bigger than Jack's cottage! The giant ate his fill, then slumped into a deep sleep.

The giant's snores rumbled
around the castle. Jack summoned up all
his courage and crept out of the cupboard.

"Those gold coins would feed us for a hundred years!"
he gasped.

"They belong to you," whispered the giant's wife.
She explained in a hushed voice that her husband had
stolen a great deal of money from Jack's father
many years before.

While the giant slept on, Jack dragged a heavy money bag out of the castle and back down the beanstalk.

When Jack got to the bottom of the beanstalk, he ran inside and presented the gold coins to his mother.

"You have saved us from ruin, son!" she cried.

Time passed, but Jack still thought about the giant and his stolen treasures. So one day, despite his mother's pleading, he climbed back up the beanstalk. When he got to the castle, he could hear the giant shouting out:

"Fee-fi-fo-fum,
I smell the blood of an Englishman.
Be he alive or be he dead,
I'll grind his bones to make my bread!"

Jack hid in a cupboard again. This time, the giant was sitting at the kitchen table, holding a magic hen.

Jack waited until the giant ate his supper and fell asleep. Booming snores echoed across the kitchen.

"I must take that hen to my mother," the boy decided. "It can lay golden eggs!"

Jack led the animal back down the beanstalk. His mother was thrilled with her new hen.

The next day, Jack climbed the beanstalk again. The giant's wife looked frightened when she saw him. Her husband's shouts rumbled behind her.

"Fee-fi-fo-fum,
I smell the blood of an Englishman.
Be he alive or be he dead,
I'll grind his bones to make my bread!"

Jack hid as the giant stormed inside, setting a magic harp on the table.

As soon as the giant had fallen asleep, Jack came out of his hiding place and took the magic harp. To his horror, the harp began to speak!

"Master! Master!" it shouted.

Jack grabbed the harp, then ran out of the door.

"Hurry!" screeched the giant's wife. "You've woken up my husband!"

"Fee-fi-fo-fum!" roared the angry giant.

Jack climbed down the beanstalk as fast as he could. Up above him the giant was also clambering down the branches.

By the time Jack reached the cottage, the giant was almost upon him. As soon as her son's feet touched the grass, Jack's mother started to hack at the beanstalk with an axe.

"Stand back!" she cried, as the towering plant crashed to the ground.

The furious giant fell down dead, crushed by the enormous beanstalk.

The magic beans had restored Jack's family fortune. Now that they had what was rightfully theirs, Jack and his mother lived in peace and contentment for the rest of their days. Neither of them would ever be hungry again.

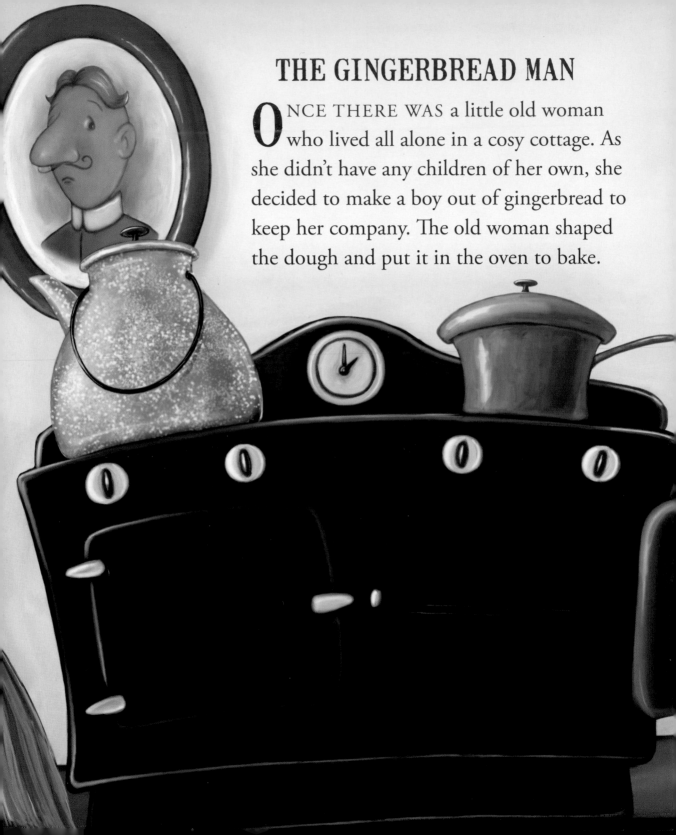

THE GINGERBREAD MAN

ONCE THERE WAS a little old woman who lived all alone in a cosy cottage. As she didn't have any children of her own, she decided to make a boy out of gingerbread to keep her company. The old woman shaped the dough and put it in the oven to bake.

Soon a delicious aroma wafted through the old woman's kitchen. Her little Gingerbread Man was ready.

"You've browned nicely," said the woman, taking him out of the oven.

To her surprise, the Gingerbread Man sat up and looked at her. The old woman gasped as he jumped down, ran out of the kitchen and straight down the garden path.

The old woman reached for her rolling pin.

"Stop!" she cried, running down the path in her slippers. "You belong to me!"

The Gingerbread Man turned back and laughed at her.

"Run, run, as fast as you can,
You can't catch me,
I'm the Gingerbread Man!"

The little Gingerbread Man scampered out of the garden. He grinned with mischief when he saw the old woman struggling up the lane behind him. He ran on and on towards the forest at the top of the hill.

"Come back now!" begged the old woman, stopping to catch her breath. She shouted and waved her rolling pin, but the Gingerbread Man gave the same answer:

"Run, run, as fast as you can,
You can't catch me,
I'm the Gingerbread Man!"

With that, he turned on his heel and disappeared into the leafy forest.

A few moments later, the Gingerbread Man met a cow.

"Stop!" shouted the cow. "I want to eat you for my tea."

The Gingerbread Man threw back his head and laughed.

"Run, run, as fast as you can,
You can't catch me,
I'm the Gingerbread Man!"

The cow chased after the Gingerbread Man. The old woman ran along too, waving her rolling pin at the little fellow.

"Come back now!" screeched the old woman.

The Gingerbread Man kept on running. The cow and the old woman called and called, but they could not catch him.

The path twisted and turned, until the Gingerbread Man finally spotted a farm up ahead.

His plump currant eyes twinkled as he stopped to wave at the cow and the old woman.

"Run, run, as fast as you can,
You can't catch me,
I'm the Gingerbread Man!"

When he got to the farm, the Gingerbread Man met a horse.

"Stop!" shouted the horse. "I want to eat you for my tea."

The Gingerbread Man only grinned.

"Run, run, as fast as you can,
You can't catch me,
I'm the Gingerbread Man!"

The horse cantered after the Gingerbread Man,
closely followed by the cow and the old woman.
  "Come back now!" puffed the old woman.
  But the Gingerbread Man kept on running.
Neither the horse, the cow, nor the old
woman could catch him.

However, the Gingerbread Man had to stop running when he came to the edge of a river. A fox stepped up to meet him.

"Jump on to my tail," said the sneaky fox. "I will help you get to the other side."

The Gingerbread Man hopped on to the fox's bushy tail and held on tightly.

The horse, the cow and the old woman watched as the fox began to swim over the river.

Soon though, the Gingerbread Man felt his little feet dipping in the water.

"Jump on to my back," said the fox, "then your feet won't get wet."

The Gingerbread Man slowly crawled on to the fox's red back. At first, the soft fur felt warm and dry.

When they got a little deeper, splashes of water started to soak the Gingerbread Man's toes.

"Jump on to my head," said the fox, "then your feet won't get wet."

The fox licked his lips as the Gingerbread Man edged closer and closer.

The water swirled below the Gingerbread Man. The fox's eyes darted left and right as he swam towards the bank.

The Gingerbread Man took a deep
breath, then leapt on to the
fox's head.

SNAP!

The fox tossed the Gingerbread Man into the
air and swallowed him down in one. His sly trick
had worked!

The horse, the cow and the old woman stood
on the bank and stared. That was the end of their
proud little Gingerbread Man.

THE PIED PIPER OF HAMELIN

A LONG TIME AGO, there was a beautiful little town called Hamelin. The people of the town lived in peace and harmony for many years. Harvests were good and the citizens prospered. There was music and dancing from dawn to dusk.

But one day, everything in Hamelin changed.

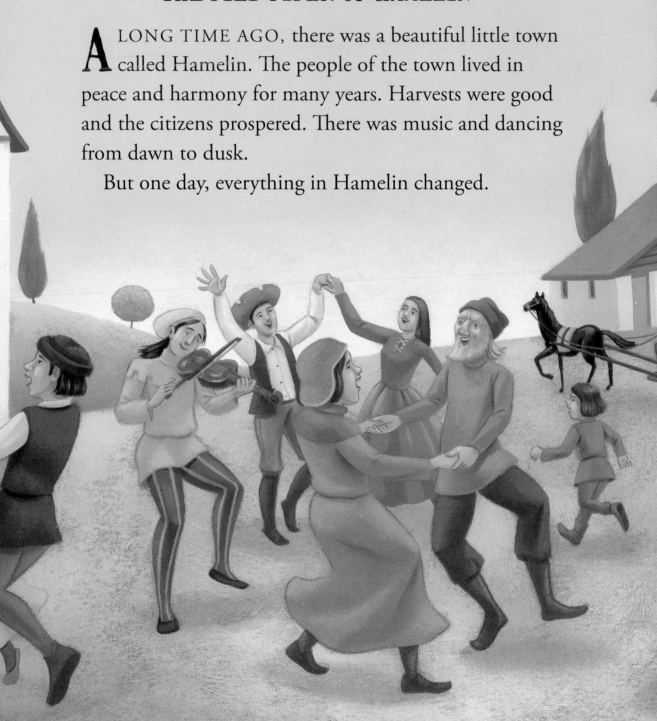

Thousands and thousands of rats suddenly ran into the town.

There were big rats and little rats, thin rats and fat rats. The plague of beasts scratched their way into houses and swarmed through the streets.

By nightfall, not a single corner in Hamelin was untouched
by the rats.

The plague of rats drove the townspeople wild.

"There are rats on my table!" cried one man.

"There are rats in my boots!" shouted another.

Women ran from their kitchens in terror. Great black rats scurried into their store cupboards and swarmed over their food.

Children cried and held each other. All the while rats nibbled their playthings and tugged at their clothes.

Night-times were even worse. Bands of rats darted across the bedclothes and scratched on the floorboards all over town.

"There are rats in my bed!" sobbed one little girl.

"There are rats on the roof!" shrieked her brother.

Hamelin was filled with the sound of gnawing and thousands of scuttling feet.

The people put out traps and prayed for the rats to go away, but nothing worked.

The citizens of Hamelin rushed out to find
the mayor.

"Get rid of these rats!" shouted the crowd.

The mayor held out his hands in despair.

"What can I do?" he asked. "There are rats
in my house too."

A few days later a stranger asked to see the mayor. The curious fellow was dressed from head to foot in red and yellow. He was carrying a fluted pipe.

"I am the Pied Piper," he smiled. "I can make the rats go away, if you pay me a thousand silver coins."

Even though he knew this was a small fortune, the mayor agreed. He would do anything to rid the town of this terrible plague of rats!

"Don't forget your promise," warned the Pied Piper, sweeping out of the door.

The mayor watched from his window as the stranger walked across the main square. Then the Pied Piper began to play a curious tune.

Rats streamed out of the houses and shops, enchanted by the melody.

The Pied Piper walked towards the river, still playing the strange tune on his pipe. The streets of Hamelin turned black with a torrent of deserting rats.

The plague swept its way to the riverbank. Rat after rat tumbled into the waters, never to be seen again.

When every rat had perished, the Pied Piper returned for his payment.

"I've nothing for you," declared the mayor. The foolish man sent the Pied Piper away without paying him a single penny.

"Now I will play another tune," vowed the stranger. "And you will not be so happy with the result!"

The Pied Piper walked out on to the streets. He began to play a new refrain on his pipe. This melody was even more haunting than the last.

In all the houses and in all the streets of Hamelin, the children stopped playing. One by one, they ran after the Pied Piper.

The people called to their children to stop, but they didn't
seem to hear. The children followed the Pied Piper through
the town and over the river.

The Pied Piper led the enchanted children towards
a great mountain.

Suddenly an entrance appeared in the rock. All
the children of Hamelin skipped inside.

The Pied Piper danced on, leading the children to
a beautiful land blooming with trees and flowers.

Only one little boy didn't disappear into the mountainside.
The child had hurt his leg and could only hobble on crutches.
He saw his friends go into the mountain, but he was too slow
to follow them.

The little boy made his way back to the town. The mayor ran
up to him, his face filled with panic.

"My friends are inside a mountain with the Pied Piper,"
cried the boy. "They will never come back."

The townspeople stormed into the market square.
Furious mothers and fathers pointed their fingers
and shook their fists at the mayor.

"Where are our children?" they demanded.

The mayor hung his head in shame.

"You must find them!" shouted the villagers.
"Bring our little ones back to us!"

The mayor fled the town at once, ashamed
by his greed.

He spent years and years wandering
the mountain trails, searching for the lost
children of Hamelin. Even when he grew
old and his clothes turned to rags, he never
gave up on his quest. Some say that he is
still out there searching today.

THE THREE LITTLE PIGS

ONCE UPON A TIME, there were three little pigs who were ready to seek their fortunes.

Each little pig packed what he thought he might need. Then he set off to build a house to live in.

The first little pig built his house out of straw.

"My golden fences will be the talk of the town!" he bragged.

The second little pig built his house out of sticks.

"My timber roof looks very fine!" he boasted.

The third little pig built his house out of bricks. It took a long time to finish it.

"My brick walls are solid and strong," he said.

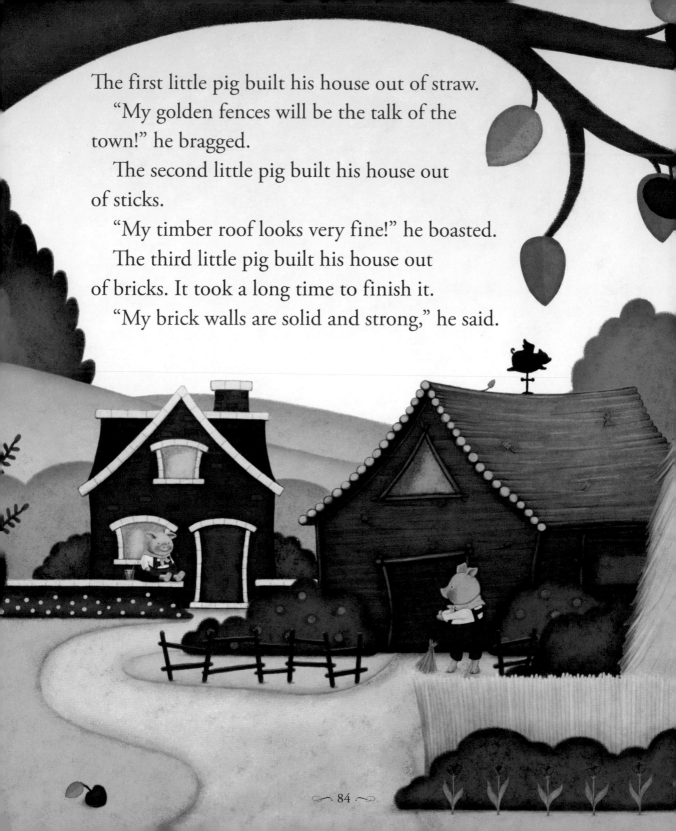

One day, a big, bad wolf stopped outside the
house of straw. A sly snarl crept over his face
when he saw who was living inside.

The wolf walked up the path then rang the
bell politely.

"Little pig, little pig, let me come in," he said.

The little pig cowered behind his front door.

"No, no," he replied. "Not by the hair of my chinny, chin, chin!"

The wolf licked his chops and rang the bell again.

The little pig heard the doorbell jingle a second time. The wolf peered in through the window.

"Then I'll huff and I'll puff and I'll blow your house in!" he threatened.

The little pig trembled with fear, but he knew that he could never let the wolf come inside.

The wolf gave a menacing roar. Then he huffed and he puffed and he blew the house in!

"Help!" cried the first little pig, as his straw house tumbled to the ground.

The frightened pig picked himself up and dashed to find shelter at the second little pig's house.

The first little pig had just arrived when the wolf turned up at the house of sticks.

"Little pig, little pig, let me come in," said the wolf.

The second little pig slid the bolt across his front door.

"No, no," he answered. "Not by the hair of my chinny, chin, chin!"

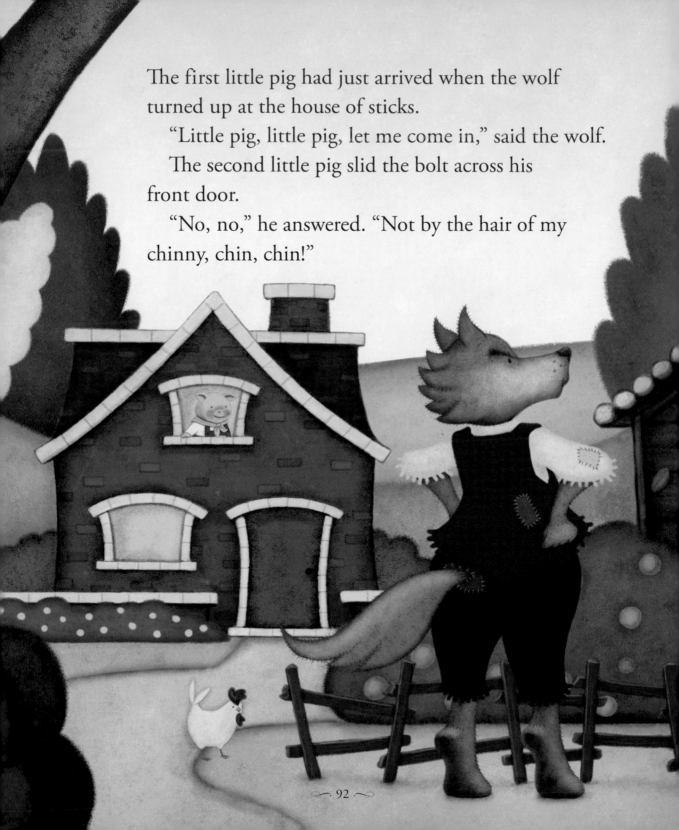

The wolf pushed hard against the little pig's stick walls.

"Then I'll huff and I'll puff and I'll blow your house in!" he warned.

The two little pigs still wouldn't open the door.

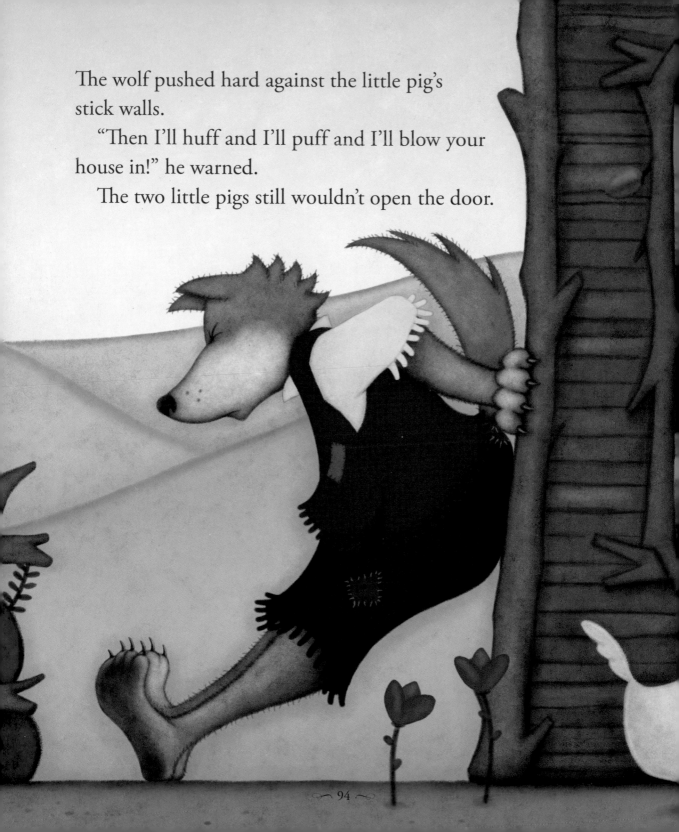

The wolf growled in anger. Then he huffed and he
puffed and he blew the house in!

"Help!" squealed the second little pig as his stick house
fell to pieces around him.

The scared pair of pigs ran to hide at the third
little pig's house.

The third little pig let his brothers in, then slammed the front door shut.

"Little pig, little pig, let me come in," urged the wolf.

"No, no," retorted the third little pig. "Not by the hair of my chinny, chin, chin!"

The wolf glared through the third little pig's windows. He paced up and down outside, his tail swishing with irritation.

"Then I'll huff and I'll puff and I'll blow your house in!" he vowed.

The first two little pigs hid underneath the rug in fright.

Instead of joining them, the third little pig sat in his favourite armchair reading the newspaper. He didn't seem the least bit scared.

The big, bad wolf got ready to knock down the house of bricks.

The wolf let out a deafening howl. Then he huffed and he puffed and he huffed and he puffed. But as hard as he tried, he could not blow the house in!

"I'll get you, little pigs!" roared the wolf. "Even if I have to climb down the chimney!"

The third little pig didn't tremble with fear. Instead he put a cooking pot full of water on the fire to boil.

The wolf squeezed himself into the brick chimney. Downstairs in the sitting room, the little pig and his brothers waited. By now the cooking pot was bubbling nicely in the fireplace.

When the wolf came down the chimney, the third little pig lifted the lid off his cooking pot. The big, bad wolf landed with a SPLASH!

The clever little pig danced with his brothers. The wolf would never bother them again.

THE ELVES AND THE SHOEMAKER

MANY YEARS AGO, there lived an honest shoemaker. His work was good, but hard times had left him desperately poor.

"This is all the leather that we have left," he told his wife one evening. "There is nothing else in my workshop."

His wife sighed. The little piece of leather was only big enough to make one pair of shoes.

The shoemaker cut out the leather, then went up
to bed with a heavy heart.

But when he came down the next morning, to his
surprise the leather had been made into a beautiful
pair of shoes.

"I've never seen such tiny stitching!" cried the
shoemaker. "They are a masterpiece."

The shoemaker and his wife placed the shoes in
their shop window.

It wasn't long before the shoes caught the eye of a very rich lady. She swept into the shop to try them on.

"They fit perfectly!" she beamed. "I have to have them."

The shoemaker hugged his wife. The lady had given them three gold coins – twice the usual price!

The lady was so thrilled with the shoes she insisted on wearing them out of the shop. Everyone stopped to admire the elegant heels and fine embroidery.

The shoemaker used the gold coins to buy some more leather. Now he had enough leather to make two new pairs of shoes.

That night, the shoemaker cut out all the pieces that he needed.

"I shall make these in the morning," he smiled, climbing the stairs to bed.

The shoemaker and his wife slept well, dreaming pleasant dreams for the first time in months.

The next morning, the shoemaker and his wife were thrilled to find two new pairs of shoes waiting for them.

"The work is perfection," marvelled the shoemaker. "Who could have done it?"

Within minutes, a rich man had come in and paid handsomely for both pairs.

Now the shoemaker had enough money to buy the leather for four pairs of shoes. That evening he sat by his candle, cutting out the patterns. As he worked, he couldn't help but wonder what he would discover the next morning.

The shoemaker wasn't disappointed. When he woke the next day, four beautiful pairs of shoes were laid in a neat row upon his worktop. Now that word had got round the town, the shoes sold in minutes.

"We must find out who is helping us," the shoemaker told his wife.

The next evening the shoemaker worked late,
cutting out enough leather for even more pairs
of shoes. This time, instead of going to bed
afterwards, he and his wife hid at the back
of the shop.

At midnight, the shop door swung open.
Two tiny elves skipped in, dressed in rags.
They jumped on the table and opened their
little green bags. Inside were tacks, needles
and thread.

The elves sewed and hammered all night. The shoemaker and his wife gasped as the tiny people stitched shoe after shoe. Each design was more eye-catching than the last.

By sunrise, the work was done. The elves picked up their bags and bustled out of the shop.

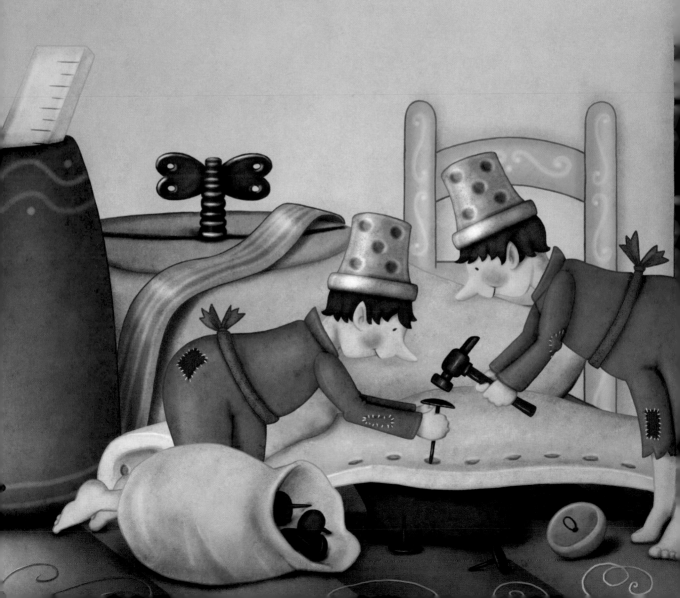

The shoemaker and his wife rubbed their eyes.

"Those little elves have saved our shop," said the shoemaker. "We must find a way of thanking them."

"The elves were dressed in rags," said his wife. "We shall make them each a brand new outfit."

The shoemaker and his wife got to work straight away.

It took all day to make the outfits. By evening, the shoemaker and his wife had made green jackets, trousers, undershirts and little hats for the elves. They'd even stitched two miniature pairs of boots.

"Everything must be perfect," said the shoemaker, laying the garments out on his worktop.

The couple smiled, then hid at the back of the shop again.

On the stroke of midnight, the shop door swung open just as it had the night before. The two elves skipped across the floor, then clambered on to the worktop.

"What is this?" cried one of them, holding up a tiny shirt.

The shoemaker and his wife smiled from their hiding place.

"These are the finest clothes I have ever seen!" declared the other.

The two elves pulled on the smart clothes. The little knitted socks, breeches and jackets all fitted a treat.

"Look at us!" laughed the elves, dancing out of the door.

The kind elves kept on helping the shoemaker and his wife. Soon the shop was filled with elegant shoes in every style and colour imaginable.

Every night, the shoemaker cut out more leather for his little friends to stitch. But now he also laid out new shirts and sweaters to keep the elves warm and comfortable too.

"What wonderful friends we have!" smiled the shoemaker.

The shoe shop became famous all across the land. The shoemaker and his wife were rich for the rest of their days, always giving thanks for the night that the elves first came to visit.

THE THREE BILLY GOATS GRUFF

ONCE UPON A TIME there were three billy goats called Gruff. The goats lived in a bleak field that stretched along a riverbank. Very little grass grew there, but on the other side of the river the land was lush and green.

"I'm hungry!" bleated the smallest billy goat Gruff.

He decided to trot over the bridge and eat the grass on the other side.

The smallest billy goat Gruff went trip-trap, trip-trap, trip-trap over the bridge. Up ahead he could see a lush meadow full of good things to eat.

Just before he got to the other side, a loud growl came from underneath the bridge. The smallest billy goat Gruff stopped.

The billy goats Gruff didn't know that it was an enchanted bridge. A fierce troll lived underneath it, eating up anybody who tried to cross over to the other side.

"What shall I do?" whispered the smallest billy goat Gruff.

When he peered over the side, he could see the troll sitting below with a fishing rod.

The troll looked grumpy and mean. He had a large red nose, wonky teeth and a shaggy black beard that was matted with knots.

"I'm hungry!" he grumbled. "What am I going to eat?"

It was several days since he'd last had a meal and he was in a very bad mood.

The smallest billy goat Gruff gulped, then made a dash for the other side.

The troll was on the bridge in an instant.

"Who's that trip-trapping over my bridge?" he yelled. "I'm going to gobble you up!"

The smallest billy goat Gruff thought fast.

"Don't eat me," he replied. "I'm only tiny. Just wait for my big brother. He's much fatter than me."

The troll rubbed his chin. At last he let the smallest billy goat Gruff go on his way.

The middle billy goat Gruff saw his little brother grazing in the lush meadow on the other side of the bridge. The grass looked green and inviting.

"I'm hungry!" the middle billy goat Gruff declared in a loud voice. He decided to cross the bridge, too.

The middle billy goat Gruff went trip-trap, trip-trap, trip-trap over the bridge. His tummy rumbled when he smelled the fresh pasture ahead.

Underneath the bridge, the troll heard every step. His eyes gleamed with excitement.

The troll leapt on to the bridge.
"Who's that trip-trapping over my bridge?"
he roared. "I'm going to gobble you up!"

The middle billy goat Gruff stepped back.
The troll blocked the bridge. He pointed a rotten
fingernail at the goat, his eyes full of menace.

The middle billy goat Gruff was just as smart as his brother. "Don't eat me," he answered. "I'm only middle-sized. Just wait for my big brother. He's much fatter than me."

The troll looked over at the biggest billy goat Gruff and licked his lips. The middle billy goat Gruff went on his way.

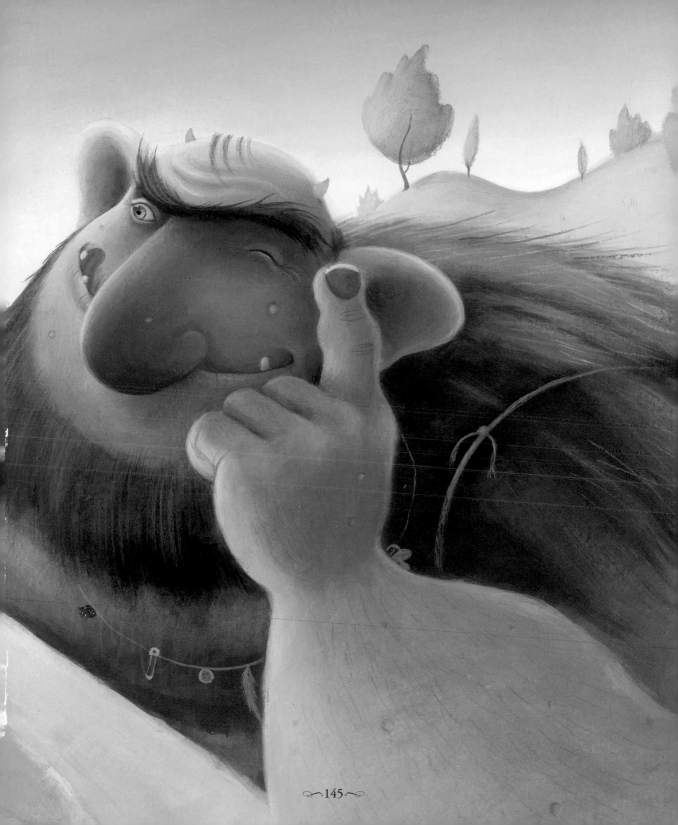

The biggest billy goat Gruff craned his neck to see how his brothers were faring. The goats were ambling lazily across the meadow on the other side of the river, eating their fill of green grass.

"I'm hungry!" he announced.

The troll grinned when he saw the biggest billy goat Gruff crossing the bridge.

The biggest billy goat Gruff went trip-trap, trip-trap, trip-trap over the bridge. He couldn't wait to have his first mouthful of fresh grass!

Suddenly, the troll hurled himself into the goat's path.

"Who's that trip-trapping over my bridge?" he boomed. "I'm going to gobble you up!"

"Oh no you're not!" shouted the biggest billy goat Gruff.

The troll dropped his knife and fork as the goat lowered his head and charged towards him.

The biggest billy goat Gruff caught the troll
with his horns and tossed him into the river.
The three brothers watched the troll land with
an enormous splash, disappearing without a trace.

"Come," smiled the biggest billy goat Gruff. "Let's go and eat our fill."

And the three billy goats Gruff grazed happily ever after.